Bamboo

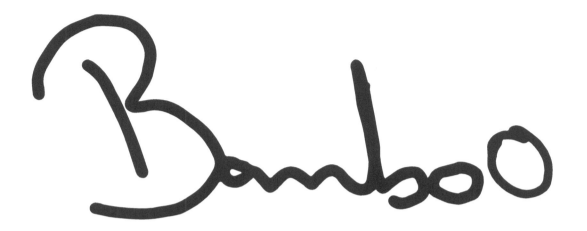

By Stephen Whitmore

This book is dedicated to Marie, Kyle, Trent, Sam & Bekah.
SW

Written and illustrated by Stephen Whitmore
Designed by Bainton House Books

For information contact:
hello@baintonhousebooks.com

First printed in the UK in 2022
ISBN 978-1-9169006-3-9

"Hello, I'm Bamboo the panda bear."

Bamboo's fur is pure white, from his head to his toes.

The other pandas and all the
animals of the forest love him so...

Especially Bamboo's mum,
who helped him to grow.

When Bamboo was little, his mum would play games with him.

She would cover his eyes with his paws and then uncover them, again and again, shouting

"Bamboo! Bamboo! Bamboo!"

The little panda bear would laugh, and his mum would too.

"Bamboo." she said one day. "That's what your name will be."

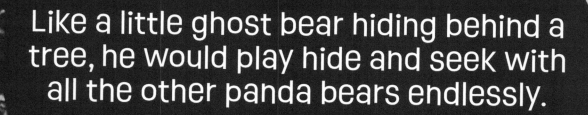

Like a little ghost bear hiding behind a tree, he would play hide and seek with all the other panda bears endlessly.

But there was one night when Bamboo strayed a little too far away...

It was one starry wintery night, when all the other panda bears were fast asleep.

Bamboo was woken up by a bright glow dancing in the forest. He crept away from his mum's arms to find out what it was.

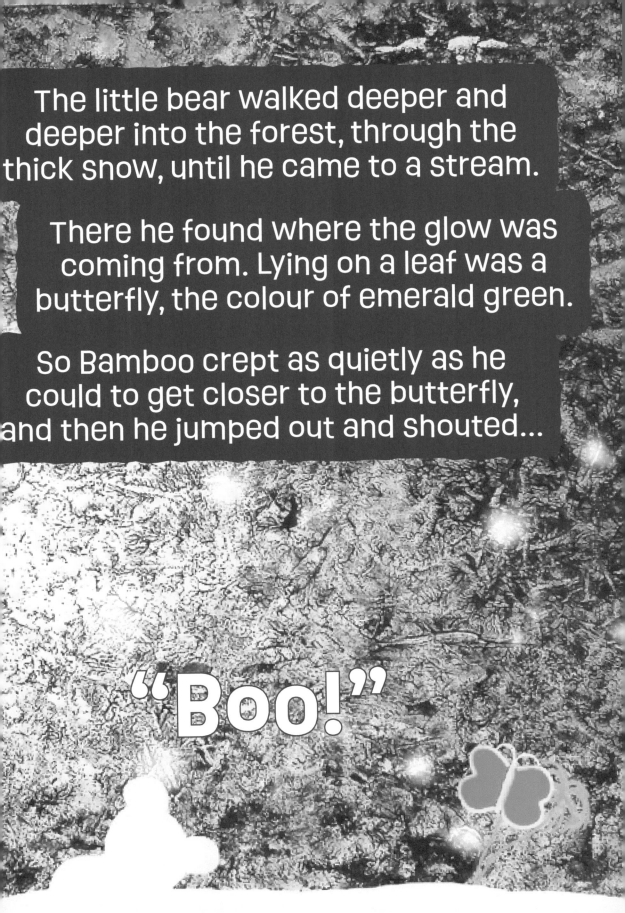

The little bear walked deeper and deeper into the forest, through the thick snow, until he came to a stream.

There he found where the glow was coming from. Lying on a leaf was a butterfly, the colour of emerald green.

So Bamboo crept as quietly as he could to get closer to the butterfly, and then he jumped out and shouted...

"Boo!"

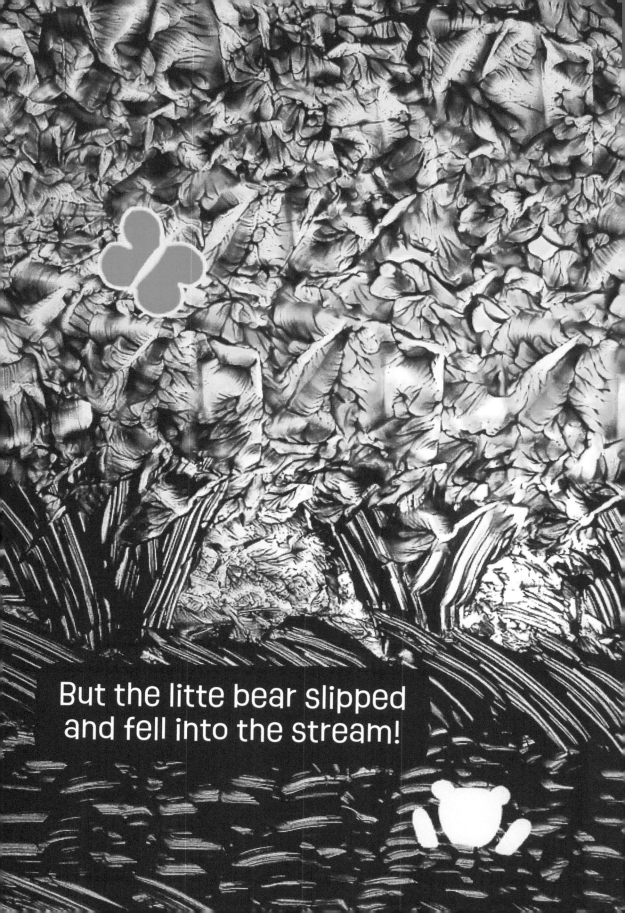

But the litte bear slipped and fell into the stream!

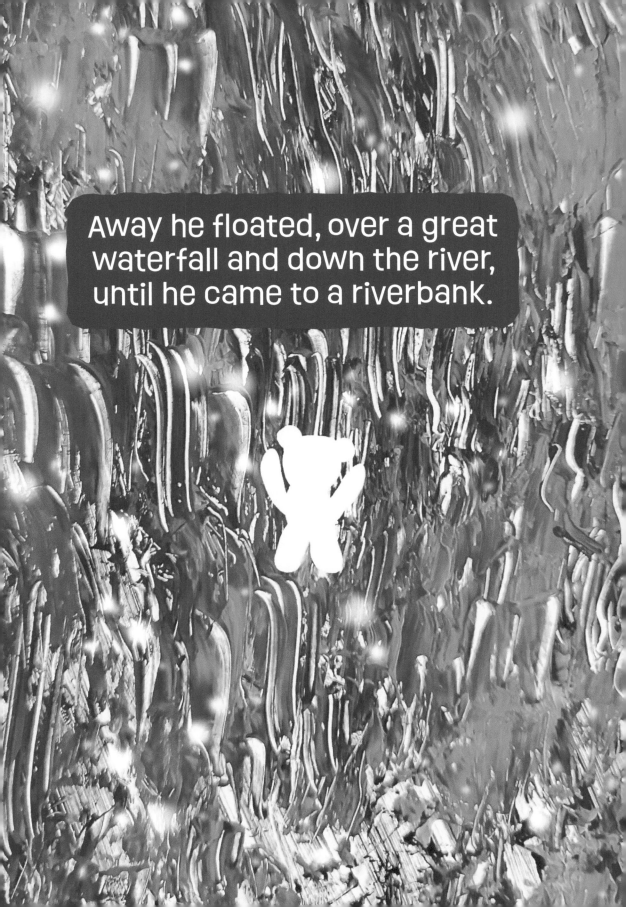

Away he floated, over a great waterfall and down the river, until he came to a riverbank.

On the riverbank he found an old broken boat.

"I'll have to sleep here tonight."
Bamboo said quietly.

His fur and body were all cold and wet through. He tried to sleep, but he was missing his home and his mum's warm and loving arms.

...and hanging from a tree was a golden crown and a beautiful red coat.

Bamboo walked over and put on the coat and the golden crown. Then suddenly he heard a deep voice ring out.

"Fit for a king, I would say!"

Bamboo slowly turned, and out of the sky a great dragon approached.

"You seem lost."
the dragon said quietly

"And I don't think that
broken boat is going
to get you home!
Maybe I can help? You
don't have to be shy,
what's your name?"

Little Bamboo slowly showed
his face and started to talk.

"My name is Bamboo," he said sadly.

"I'm lost and I miss my mum."

"I see." said the dragon.

"Well, Bamboo, my name is Shenlong. Would you like to come on an adventure with me?"

"Will you take me back home after?"
asked the little bear.

"Of course!"

smiled the dragon.

"Hop on board!"

Away the dragon flew, with little King Bamboo wearing his golden crown, and his red coat blowing in the wind...

...past every snow-topped
mountain and every small town,
and then way up into the sky...

...past the clouds, and up
and up they went!

Shenlong soared with
tremendous speed past
every star and every planet
in the whole galaxy.

"I will take you home
now, if you wish?"

asked the dragon.

"No, no!" shouted Bamboo.
"Just one last time!"

"As you wish."
laughed the dragon.

When they came back down
again, the dragon took the
little bear back home.

He safely placed
Bamboo next to the
stream where he fell.

"**NOW,**" said Shenlong, "you must get back to your mum, and if you're lucky she will still be fast asleep!"

"Can I keep the coat and the golden crown?" asked little Bamboo.

"You don't need this coat and crown, Bamboo," answered the dragon.

"You're more than a king in your mum's eyes already."

And then the
dragon was gone.

Bamboo ran back home as quickly as he could. Then he tucked himself quietly under his mum's arms and fell asleep.

In the morning Bamboo told his mum about his adventure with the great dragon Shenlong.

"What a lovely dream that sounds like, Bamboo!" she said.

"It wasn't a dream!" shouted Bamboo. "You must come and see!"

So Bamboo took his mum to the stream...

...and hanging from a tree was the beautiful red coat and the golden crown, just as the dragon had left them.

the
end

Lightning Source UK Ltd.
Milton Keynes UK
UKHW050909020822
406704UK00002B/40